Fitness Crash

written by Mari Kesselring

illustrated by Mariano Epelbaum

www.12StoryLibrary.com

Copyright © 2015 by Peterson Publishing Company, North Mankato, MN 56003. All rights reserved. No part of this book may be reproduced or utilized in any form or by any means without written permission from the publisher.

12-Story Library is an imprint of Peterson Publishing Company and Press Room Editions.

Produced for 12-Story Library by Red Line Editorial

Illustrations by Mariano Epelbaum

ISBN
978-1-63235-042-8 (hardcover)
978-1-63235-102-9 (paperback)
978-1-62143-083-4 (hosted ebook)

Library of Congress Control Number: 2014946002

Printed in the United States of America
Mankato, MN
October, 2014

Table of Contents

Out of Shape

Bridget crouched down on the track, fixing her eyes on the finish line. *It's only 100 meters,* she coached herself. *You can do this! Don't let anyone pass you!*

"Go!" shouted Coach Harrison. Bridget sprang from her spot and began to sprint as fast as she could. It was the first soccer practice of the season, and this sprint was meant to test the players' conditioning. Bridget gasped for breath as she tried to keep up with her teammates. Before she knew it, she was crossing the finish line dead last.

"Nice work, team!" Coach Harrison called out. "Now let's move on to some passing drills."

Bridget didn't feel as confident as Coach Harrison seemed to be. Last year, she had been the star forward on Interface, Blue Lake Junior

High's soccer team. She had been one of the team's top scorers, and she was fast too. She could sprint halfway down the field before the other team's defenders even knew she was on a breakaway. But that was last year.

Poua Vang breezed past Bridget.

"Looking a little slow out there, Bridget," Poua said. "Maybe we need someone else playing forward."

"No," Bridget huffed. Poua bossed everyone around, especially Bridget. Bridget was used to it since they were in art club together and Poua was the club's president. "I'm just a little out of shape. You'll see, I'll be running circles around you in a week or two."

"I hope so," Poua said. "Or we won't be any good this year."

Bridget tried to ignore the pangs of anxiety in her stomach. Why did she seem so much slower this year? Bridget looked around at her teammates practicing, and suddenly she realized: everyone was taller.

Last year, Bridget had been one of the taller kids at school. But over the school year, her teammates had shot up like weeds. Some of them now towered over Bridget, and their long legs rippled with muscle. Bridget glanced down at her short, skinny legs. They looked like twigs.

Bridget sighed. Usually she kept active during the winter months to stay in shape for soccer season in the spring. But this past year she'd spent a lot of time at her computer working on blog posts for Tech Club and hadn't gotten much exercise. Her teammates must have been spending all their free time working out.

Bridget pulled her smartphone out of her back pocket and glanced around warily. Coach allowed smartphones at practice so kids could listen to music during warm-ups, but after warm-ups they were strictly forbidden. Bridget knew the rule, but since she was totally obsessed with all things technology, she sometimes had trouble following it. Bridget activated the voice control as she raised her smartphone to her mouth and whispered, "Text Emma." Emma Hein was Bridget's best friend.

"Way too slow at soccer. Want to train together?" Bridget whispered into her phone, and then added, "Send text."

Emma's response was almost immediate. *Sure! I could use some conditioning 4 dance team.*

Bridget smiled. She reached down discreetly to slip her smartphone back into her pocket, but she nearly fumbled it when Coach Harrison blew the whistle.

"Okay, team!" Coach shouted. "That's it for today! Have a great weekend."

As the players headed inside toward the locker room, Bridget felt a tap on her shoulder. She turned to see her teammate Carmina Torres. Like many of the others, Carmina had definitely grown since last soccer season. She was nearly a head taller than Bridget.

"Hey, Bridget!" Carmina said casually. "Fun practice, huh? That pass you made to Poua was awesome."

Bridget shrugged. "Yeah, I guess."

"Hey," Carmina said, frowning. "What's wrong?"

"Last year I beat everyone in sprints on day one," Bridget pointed out.

"Maybe you need to work on conditioning?" Carmina suggested.

"Yeah, definitely."

"Do you have a FitLife?" Carmina held her wrist out to Bridget. Bridget studied the pink, rubbery bracelet on Carmina's wrist. "I got one to help me with my conditioning. I hope to start this year. FitLife syncs to your smartphone and . . ."

Bridget was nodding. She knew about FitLife.

"Oh yeah," Carmina said, looking embarrassed. "Lingo makes it. Doesn't your dad, like, own that company?"

"He's the president," Bridget replied. Lingo, the local tech company run by her dad, Nick Grant, was known for its cutting-edge products. Bridget owned many of Lingo's gadgets, but she had never thought about using FitLife before. Running and soccer had always been fairly easy for her. But now it looked like she needed help keeping up with her teammates. She always loved using tech gadgets. Maybe FitLife could help motivate her to exercise more.

"That's not a bad idea," Bridget said.

"Worth a try!" Carmina said. "We should be workout buddies."

Bridget hesitated. She liked Carmina, but she already had a workout buddy—Emma.

"That would be great . . . except I already promised I was going to start working out with Emma."

"Oh well! Never mind," Carmina said with a smile.

As they walked past the basketball court at the end of the track, Carmina suddenly blushed red. A bunch of guys were playing a pickup game on the court. Bridget looked at Carmina quizzically.

"Do you know Mark Ellison?" Carmina whispered. "He's just so cute. I have the biggest crush on him."

Bridget glanced over at the court just in time to see Mark make a basket. Of course Bridget knew who he was. Mark was one of the most popular guys at Blue Lake. Nearly every girl had a crush on him. She felt her face get hot and hoped she wasn't blushing as obviously as Carmina.

"Uh, yeah," Bridget said, suddenly feeling awkward. "He's cute."

Carmina waved her hand in front of her face, fanning herself. "He's so awesome."

Bridget nodded, trying to act as if she couldn't care less.

"Well, good luck with the FitLife," Carmina said as she headed toward her locker. "I bet it will help you a lot."

"I hope so," Bridget said. She texted her dad, *Can I have a FitLife 4 soccer? PLEASE?*

2

Upgraded

Bridget knew there was a good chance her dad would get her a FitLife. But it would cost her. She'd have to contribute a few months of allowance or do extra chores. Even though her dad was president of Lingo, he would never just hand out free gadgets to Bridget. He made her work for them.

Sure enough, by the time she'd biked home, Bridget had a text from her dad.

I'll bring one home for you tonight. But it will cost you two months of allowance.

Bridget groaned aloud. *Two whole months of allowance?* She glanced over at the soccer trophy on top of her bedroom dresser. Last year, she'd helped lead Blue Lake's soccer team to the semifinals. Bridget couldn't let her team down, and she couldn't let what Poua said be true. She wasn't losing her edge. Bridget texted her dad: *Deal.*

Less than an hour later, Bridget's dad arrived home. From the doorway, he tossed Bridget a white box with the blue Lingo logo on the side.

"Dad! Be careful!" Bridget yelped, catching the box.

Bridget's dad just laughed. "This isn't like your other gadgets. You don't need to be so careful with it."

Bridget opened the box and pulled out the FitLife bracelet. He'd picked out a purple one—Bridget's favorite color.

"This is so awesome!" Bridget said, fastening the bracelet to her wrist.

"Start by syncing it with your smartphone. Then the app will automatically download. Use the app to . . ."

"Yeah, yeah, Dad," Bridget interrupted him, rolling her eyes. "I think I can figure it out." Kids at school didn't call her Bridget Gadget for nothing.

"Okay, sure—just let me know if you have any questions," her dad said, but she was already working on setting up her FitLife.

"It's perfect," Bridget said. "This is exactly what I need to motivate myself."

"Why do you need this again?" Bridget's dad asked as he poured himself a glass of water. "For soccer?"

"Yeah," Bridget said absently. "I was just a little lazy all winter. So I have to work on my endurance."

Creases appeared in Bridget's dad's forehead as he listened to her.

"Just make sure you don't overdo it."

"What do you mean?" Bridget asked.

"Don't set unattainable fitness goals. Just be healthy, okay?"

Bridget scowled. Her dad worried way too much. "Of course, Dad," she said. "I'm not going to turn into a health nut or anything."

When Bridget's smartphone alarm started beeping at 7:00 the next morning, she nearly hurled the phone across the room.

"But it's Saturday!" she protested, as if her smartphone could understand her. Suddenly the FitLife bracelet on her wrist began to vibrate. She had set the alarm on her FitLife too and worn it to bed. There was no way she'd be getting back to sleep now.

Waking up early for a run with Emma had sounded like such a good idea last night when Bridget was well rested, but now she couldn't think of a worse Saturday morning activity.

As Bridget picked up her phone to turn off the alarm, a text came in from Emma.

Cant believe u talked me into this. U better b @ the park.

Bridget scrambled to change into her workout clothes so she could meet Emma as planned. If she wanted Emma to continue running with her, she had to uphold her end of the bargain.

Emma was waiting, stretching her legs on the seat of the picnic table, when Bridget arrived at the park.

"You're late, Gadget!" Emma exclaimed.

"Sorry! Not used to getting up this early on a Saturday." Bridget consulted the FitLife app on her phone. She had to get in just one mile in under ten minutes to reach her exercise goal for the day. "Let's run!"

Emma rolled her eyes, and they took off running.

After a few laps around the park, Bridget pressed the button on her FitLife to hear her progress.

"Zero-point-five miles completed. Miles to goal: zero-point-five," the FitLife said.

Only half a mile left! Bridget thought. *I can totally do this.*

But then Bridget realized that Emma was no longer running at her side. She glanced back to see her friend struggling to keep up with her pace. Bridget slowed down to wait for her.

"Are we done yet?" Emma gasped.

3

Motivation Fail

"You're tired?" Bridget asked.

"Yeah, exhausted!" Emma whined. "My feet hurt too. I thought you said this was going to be fun!"

"Well . . ." Bridget didn't know what to say. She enjoyed running and pushing herself to meet her fitness goals. Sure, it wasn't easy, but Bridget felt good about challenging herself, and the FitLife would help keep her motivated. It was pretty clear that Emma didn't feel the same way.

Emma wiped sweat from her forehead and gave Bridget a look of desperation.

"Can we stop to rest for a second?" Emma asked, slowing her pace down to a walk as she eyed a nearby picnic table.

Bridget wanted to keep going. How was she going to meet her goals if they stopped every half mile to rest? But Bridget didn't want to leave Emma behind either.

"Okay," Bridget said, following Emma to the picnic table.

Emma flung herself down dramatically.

"I think I'm gonna die," Emma gasped, laughing a little. "Seriously, why did we do this so early?"

Bridget shrugged. She pressed the button on her FitLife.

"Miles to goal: zero-point-five," Bridget frowned. She wasn't going to fail on her first fitness goal.

"What is that?" Emma asked, pointing at the bracelet.

Bridget perked up. Maybe if Emma got a FitLife, she'd be more motivated too.

"It's a FitLife," Bridget said. "It tracks my fitness goals and helps keep me motivated. It's really cool." Bridget held out her arm so Emma could look at the bracelet. "You should get one!"

"How much was it?" Emma asked.

"It cost me two months' allowance."

"Two whole months?" Emma's mouth hung open. "For a device that makes you exercise more? That's dumb."

"It'll be worth it, though," Bridget explained, "when I'm the top scorer on our soccer team."

Emma just readjusted her ponytail and rested her head on the picnic table.

"Are you rested enough to start running again?" Bridget asked, already sensing what Emma's answer would be.

"Ugh," Emma grunted. "Do we have to? I have an idea. Let's run over to the Cyber Hills Web Café and get some coffee coolers to reward ourselves."

Bridget sighed. The Cyber Hills Web Café was only a couple of blocks away. She wouldn't meet her fitness goal for the day with a light run there. Plus, Bridget wanted to eat healthy and avoid sugars and caffeine—things those coffee coolers were loaded with.

But then Bridget looked at her friend. Emma had her eyes closed as she rested her head on the table. Strands of blonde hair stuck to her sweaty forehead. It wasn't Emma's fault that running wasn't really her thing. Plus, getting coffee coolers did sound like fun.

Bridget smiled. "Sure," she said. "Let's do it."

"Really?" Emma jumped up excitedly. "I'll race you there!" she said as she took off running.

Bridget dashed after her.

After Bridget and Emma got their coffee coolers at the Cyber Hills Web Café, they walked back to Bridget's house.

"You wanna play video games or something?" Emma asked as they arrived.

"Yeah, that'd be fun—"

Suddenly, a new message alert popped up on Emma's smartphone.

"Uh-oh," Emma said, looking down at the message. "My mom just texted me. I was supposed to clean my room today. I'd better get home."

"Okay," Bridget said, a little disappointed. "Thanks for running with me!"

"No problem! Let's do it again tomorrow!"

Bridget couldn't hide the surprise on her face. "I thought you hated it," Bridget said.

"Well, it wasn't easy, but it's fun to hang out," Emma said. "So, tomorrow?"

"Yeah, okay," Bridget said, frowning. *But what if Emma wanted to get a coffee cooler again?* she worried.

"Great!" Emma said as she headed down Bridget's driveway to walk home. "See you at seven!"

As Emma disappeared around the street corner, Bridget consulted the FitLife app on her smartphone. She was still nearly half a mile away from her fitness goal for the day. Bridget thought about running more, but the coffee cooler sat in her stomach like a rock. She'd have to try again later.

4

A Challenge

"Grant!" Coach Harrison called Bridget's last name as the Interface players rounded the final lap of their endurance run at practice that Monday. Bridget was lagging behind the rest of the team. "Pick it up, Grant!"

Bridget pumped her legs hard, gasping as she tried to catch up. Last year, she'd never been last during any of the runs. Bridget hated looking at all her teammates' backs as they raced ahead of her. She especially disliked seeing Poua's long ponytail flapping up ahead like a little banner.

As the first girls in the group crossed the finish line and transitioned into a slow jog to cool down, Bridget couldn't help but notice that Carmina had crossed the line first.

When Bridget finally crossed the line herself, behind the rest of her teammates, she felt like crying. How could she play forward if she was the slowest one on the team?

"Saw you struggling a bit," Coach Harrison said, clapping a hand on Bridget's back. "Did you do any preseason conditioning?"

Bridget hung her head. "Well, no, not much," she said. "But I'm doing some workouts outside of practice now to catch up."

Coach Harrison nodded. "Great, but don't overdo it. And let me know if you need any help coming up with a healthy workout plan."

"Sure, Coach," Bridget said, frowning as Coach walked away.

Poua snuck up behind Bridget.

"Uh, Bridget," Poua said, flipping her ponytail over her shoulder. "I need at least a regional championship in junior high if I can expect to play varsity in high school. If you can't do it, we need to have someone else play forward."

Bridget pretended not to hear. The thought of losing her spot to someone else made her stomach turn. But Bridget knew Poua was right. Forward was an important position.

The team depended on her, and she had to improve fast.

On their next run, Bridget had tried to slow down to Emma's pace, hoping that would encourage Emma to keep going. No such luck. Emma had wanted to stop at the exact same picnic table they'd ended at on Saturday. Meanwhile, Bridget's FitLife gave her negative progress remarks and constantly reminded her to complete her fitness goals. The whole thing was depressing.

Bridget knew there was only one thing to do. She needed a new fitness partner.

At the end of practice that day, as the players headed to the locker room, Bridget jogged over to Carmina.

"Hey!" Bridget said brightly. "Great run today."

"Yeah," Carmina smiled. "I see you got a FitLife!" Carmina pointed to Bridget's purple bracelet. "Good call. Isn't it the best?"

"Yeah, I love it." Bridget said. "Do you run in the mornings?"

"Yep, every morning," Carmina said. "I like to go before it gets too hot out."

"Well, I was wondering if you'd want to run with me?"

Carmina looked confused. "But I thought you already had a workout buddy. Emma Hein, right? She's your friend?"

Bridget hesitated. She knew Emma would not be happy if Bridget replaced her, but then again, Emma would never have to find out.

"Yeah, Emma's great, but I need to step it up a notch," Bridget said. "I'd love to run with you because I think we could push each other."

"Totally. You know what would be really fun?" Carmina said.

"What?" Bridget asked, barely keeping the excitement out of her voice. She had the fastest Interface player working out with her. She'd be back up to top speed in no time.

"With FitLife, you can set up a competition between you and another FitLife user. We could compete with each other to reach our fitness goals. I did it with my cousin over the winter. It's a great motivator."

Bridget hesitated. Carmina was already in way better shape than Bridget. Competing with her would be pretty tough. But Bridget needed a challenge to start meeting her FitLife goals.

"That'd be great," Bridget said. "I'm really looking to improve."

"It's a deal then," Carmina said. "Let's start first thing tomorrow. Can I choose the path? I have a route I like to take that goes right by the basketball court where Mark plays in the mornings." Carmina blushed again. "It's great motivation."

Bridget smiled. "Sure!"

On her walk home from soccer practice, Bridget wrote to Emma,

Im done running in the a.m. Hope that's cool.

Bridget hesitated for a second before sending the text message. She knew she shouldn't lie to her best friend. But she was worried about hurting Emma's feelings. Bridget knew how bad it felt to be the slowest runner on the soccer team. She didn't want to make

Emma feel bad for being slow too. Plus, it wasn't like Emma would ever know that Bridget was running with Carmina. Bridget couldn't imagine Emma running on her own. She pressed "Send."

Emma texted back, *That's a relief. No prob. What bout meeting up @ Web Café 4 coolers instead?*

I wish, Bridget texted back. *No sweets until after soccer season.*

BORING ;-), Emma texted.

Bridget smiled. Everything was working out perfectly.

5

Pushing

Just minutes into her first run with Carmina, Bridget wondered if she'd made a mistake. Carmina ran fast—very fast. Bridget understood how Emma must have felt when running with her.

Carmina, noticing that Bridget lagged a little, turned around and jogged backward. "Come on, Grant!" she called. "You're our forward. You can do this!"

Gasping for air as she tried to catch up, Bridget fought the urge to give Carmina a punch on the nose. But at the same time, she felt grateful to have someone pushing her for a change. Just when she thought she couldn't take another stride, her FitLife started beeping.

"*Personal fitness goal complete! Good job!*" the bracelet said.

Bridget felt the thrill of accomplishment wash over her and renew her energy. She'd finally achieved a fitness goal, and it felt great. But if she wanted to beat Carmina at their fitness competition, she had to keep going. They'd set up the competition to compare their total miles traveled at a running speed. Their bracelets automatically tracked the miles they ran and alerted them about who was in the lead.

"Mark plays basketball up here at this court," Carmina called out over her shoulder. "Look strong," she advised.

Bridget thought that if she looked anything other than completely exhausted she'd be lucky. But she did her best to lengthen her strides and caught up with Carmina.

They raced past Mark and a few other boys playing basketball. Bridget looked back over her shoulder as they passed.

"I don't think they noticed us!" Bridget gasped. "They weren't even looking."

Carmina rolled her eyes and elbowed Bridget lightly. "Don't look at them! You don't want Mark to see us staring, do you?"

When Bridget got home after her run with Carmina, her dad was home.

"Whoa!" he said when he saw her walk into the house dripping with sweat. "Did you go for a run?"

"Yeah," Bridget gasped. "I'm gonna be so fast."

Bridget's dad's forehead crinkled again, and Bridget braced herself for the lecture.

"Remember when we talked about not overdoing it?"

"Yes," Bridget said between gulps of water. "I'm not."

"Okay, just be sure to pace yourself a little."

"I know. I'm just doing this fitness competition with Carmina," Bridget said. "She's really fast. Plus, we have our first soccer game on Friday. I've gotta be ready."

"Who's Carmina? And what's the competition about?"

"A friend from soccer." Bridget felt seriously annoyed by all the questions. She wasn't doing anything wrong. "Dad, I promise, I'm not going to overdo it."

"Okay, okay," Bridget's dad said. "Now just stop sweating all over the floor."

"Dad!" Bridget said louder than she meant to. "I'm gonna go shower," she muttered as she headed up the stairs. She knew her dad was just trying to help, but it annoyed her that he didn't seem to trust her at all.

That Friday, Carmina and Bridget decided to do a lighter run in the morning since they had a soccer game after school.

"You're getting faster, Grant!" Carmina said about halfway through their run.

"Still not as fast as you!" Bridget admitted. Bridget was slightly behind Carmina in the total number of miles run. Carmina sometimes ran after practice, which was keeping her in the lead.

"But you're getting there!"

"I just hope I can come through for everyone in the game tonight," Bridget said.

"You'll be great," Carmina said.

"It's just that—" Bridget started.

"Bridget!" a familiar voice yelled from somewhere behind them, interrupting Bridget. Bridget glanced over her shoulder. What she saw shocked her so much that she almost tripped over her own feet.

It was Emma, turning the corner and strolling onto the running path, coffee cooler in hand.

This is going to be bad, Bridget thought as she slowed her pace.

"Uh, you go ahead," Bridget said to Carmina. "I gotta talk to Emma. I don't want to slow you down."

"Thanks," Carmina puffed. "Catch up if you can!"

Yeah right, Bridget thought to herself. She turned around as Emma walked up to her. She appeared to be returning from a trip to the Cyber Hills Web Café.

"Why didn't you tell me you were going for a run today?" Emma said when she got closer to Bridget. "I would've come with you!"

"Um, the thing is . . ." Bridget didn't know what to say. "I started running with Carmina because, well, she's more my pace."

"What? Are you kidding me?" Emma said, looking at Bridget with obvious disbelief. "I'm too slow for you. Is that it?"

"Emma, you don't understand," Bridget said. "You aren't in soccer. I need to get a lot faster and work on my endurance if I'm going to be any good this year. I need someone to push me."

"I thought that's what your stupid bracelet was for," Emma said cuttingly. "Whatever. Have fun with your new friend." Emma turned to head back in the other direction.

"No, Emma, it's not like that," Bridget tried to explain. But Emma ran away through the park, and for once, Bridget felt too tired to keep up with her.

6

Sidelined

Halfway through the soccer game that afternoon, Bridget felt exhausted. Ever since she'd started running with Carmina, it seemed like soccer was getting harder, not easier.

Now, Bridget approached Willow Pond's goal, dribbling the ball and advancing forward. She swept the ball to the side as she avoided a midfielder.

"Nice ball control!" Coach Harrison yelled from the sidelines. "Keep with it!"

Encouraged, Bridget raced toward the goal, but one of Willow Pond's defenders was on her before she even knew what was happening. Bridget tried to dodge again, but she was so fatigued that she nearly stumbled

over her own feet. The defender stole the ball and promptly passed it to a midfielder.

Exhausted and defeated, Bridget leaned forward, resting her hands on her knees. When she straightened back up, the field seemed to shake and sway. She staggered and gained her footing again.

During the next break in the action, Coach Harrison yelled, "Substitution. Torres in. Grant out!"

"What?" Bridget felt as if she might explode. Coach Harrison wanted her off the field, and they were less than halfway through the game. Was she really playing that poorly?

"I saw you gasping for breath out there. You okay?" Coach Harrison asked. Then he turned to Carmina, who had been sitting on the sidelines. "You're in at forward."

Carmina smiled a little, but then looking at Bridget, she frowned and mouthed, "Sorry."

Bridget nodded. She understood that Carmina had to follow what Coach Harrison told her. Still, it seemed so unfair. Bridget had always been the team's forward, and one shaky game shouldn't change that. Why was she coming out already?

"Coach," Bridget said. "Keep me in! I can—"

"Bridget, Carmina deserves a chance to get in the game, and you're exhausted." Coach said firmly. Bridget plopped down in the grass and wanted to cry, but she didn't know if it was because she had been taken out of the game or because of how much her muscles ached. She'd been a mess on the field, and she knew it. Her legs were sore, and she'd been distracted thinking about how she'd hurt Emma's feelings.

Bridget wiped her sweaty hair from her face, feeling truly miserable. She'd trained so hard, and now she was on the bench. Plus, her best friend hated her. Nothing was going right.

After the game, Bridget sat in the locker room while her teammates hurried out to meet their families. Carmina had scored two goals and they'd won the game, but Bridget didn't feel happy.

Carmina patted Bridget on the shoulder. "I'm really sorry about what happened. You know I didn't ask Coach to put me in like that, right?"

"I know," Bridget said, trying to smile. "You did great."

"Thanks. I've gotta go meet my mom. See you for a run tomorrow morning?"

"Of course," Bridget said, attempting to sound like her usual self.

"Hang in there," Carmina said as she left the locker room. Bridget heard a chorus of cheers from her teammates as Carmina stepped out into the hallway.

Bridget opened the FitLife app on her smartphone. She'd been meeting her fitness goals, but it still wasn't enough. She needed to push herself more if she was going to improve. Bridget changed her fitness plan from "moderate" to "intense."

Bridget waited until it was silent in the hallway before she headed out of the locker room. She didn't really want to see anyone right now. Because of his demanding job, her dad only made it to a handful of her games. For once, she was glad he'd missed a game.

As Bridget walked out of the school building, she felt her phone vibrate in her pocket. She had a text from Emma.

Heard bout the soccer game. Wanna talk?

Bridget wanted to cry. She should've known she could count on her best friend after all.

Yeah, Bridget texted. *Ur house?*

Come on ovr, Emma texted back. Then, seconds later, *Im still mad @ u* .

Bridget sighed.

I know, she texted.

7

Crash

Bridget started walking to Emma's house, which was just a few blocks from school. The light on her FitLife blinked. Bridget pressed the button to hear the message.

"Reminder. You are two miles from your fitness goal."

Two miles, even after playing soccer? Bridget thought glumly. *I guess there's a big difference between "moderate" and "intense."* Bridget felt exhausted from even the short half she'd played during the soccer game.

If I want to improve, I can't accept these excuses, she told herself. Bridget decided to sprint to Emma's instead of just walking. She took a deep breath and started to run, doing her best to ignore the pain in her legs.

At Emma's doorstep, Bridget wiped sweat from her hair and tried to catch her breath. Emma must have seen her run up because she answered the door before Bridget had a chance to ring the bell.

"Whoa," Emma said, looking at her friend. "What happened to you?"

"Nothing . . ." Bridget took a breath. "I just ran here. You know, training."

Emma looked at her as if she had two heads.

"You just played soccer. Isn't that enough of a workout?"

Bridget checked the app on her phone—still 1.5 miles to go—and shrugged. "Can I come in? Do you have water?"

"Yeah," Emma said.

After Bridget gulped down two glasses of water, Bridget and Emma hung out in Emma's room.

"You're all sweaty," Emma complained when Bridget tried to take a seat on Emma's bed like they always did. "Do you mind sitting on the floor?"

Bridget sort of did mind—she was exhausted, and it would've felt great to sit on Emma's comfy bed—but she couldn't really blame Emma. Bridget hadn't showered since before the soccer game. Sweat, mud, and grass stains streaked her arms and legs.

"I'm sorry things didn't go great for you at the game. People were posting about it on SocCircle," Emma explained, mentioning the social networking site that pretty much everyone they knew used. "Everyone's saying how amazing Carmina was."

"She is," Bridget grumbled. "She's better than me. Way faster."

"Is that why you're running with her instead of me?" Emma snapped.

"No," Bridget said, pressing her palm to her forehead. She had a killer headache coming on. "Well, kind of . . . I'm *really* sorry about that, Emma. I need to take running seriously and push myself. But I should've told you. I just didn't want to hurt your feelings."

"Well," Emma fidgeted with her hands in her lap. "You hurt my feelings anyway."

"I'm really sorry." Bridget didn't know what else she could say.

"Thanks for saying that. I guess I get it. But you still should've told me," Emma said. Then after a minute, she added, "Do you ever think you're taking the running a little too seriously?"

"No," Bridget said, wiping sweat off her brow.

"Gadget," Emma said in a serious tone. "You just sprinted to my house *after* a game. Last year, you would've been in bed with your tablet posting about the game on SocCircle."

"This year is different," Bridget countered.

"I think that thing is an unhealthy influence," Emma said finally, pointing to Bridget's FitLife bracelet.

"FitLife? No way," Bridget said. "It's helping me."

"I don't know," Emma said with concern in her voice. "I see you checking your progress on that constantly. I think you need to take it easy."

Bridget crossed her arms over her chest, annoyed. Emma sounded too much like her dad.

"It's fine," Bridget said. "I promise."

Emma sighed.

The next morning, the bracelet's vibrations woke Bridget up for her run with Carmina. Immediately, Bridget knew something didn't feel right. She felt sweaty and sick to her stomach.

Bridget stumbled out of bed and started changing into her running clothes. Her stomach churned. She wished she didn't have to run today. All she really felt like doing was lying in bed.

She checked her phone. Her dad had sent her a text when he got home last night after she went to bed.

Bridg, you feeling okay? I have the flu. Do you need anything?

Bridget checked her FitLife app. She had to run at least four miles to reach her goal for the day, but at least one extra mile if she wanted to catch up to Carmina in their FitLife competition.

No time to wimp out, Bridget told herself as she pulled on her running shoes. Bridget decided to run a few blocks before meeting Carmina at the park. It'd be great if she could catch Carmina in their competition before they met at the park. As she ran, Bridget tried to ignore the aching of her ankles and feet. She felt like she was sweating about twice as much as usual.

When Bridget got to the park, she was already breathing hard.

Carmina looked concerned when she saw Bridget. "Did you already run?" she asked.

"Just a little," Bridget admitted. She felt like she might pass out, but there was no way she'd let Carmina know that. Bridget felt her bracelet vibrate and saw the lights blinking. She pressed the button to hear the message.

"You've surpassed Carmina in the fitness challenge," the bracelet said.

Bridget raised her arms in the air like a champ.

"Woot! Woot!" she called out.

"Good job!" Carmina said. "I knew you'd catch up with me soon. Are you still up for running with me today? You don't look so hot."

"Gee, thanks," Bridget muttered sarcastically. She didn't mean to be sharp with Carmina; she just wanted to get this run over with. "I'm fine; I totally want to run."

Carmina shrugged. "Okay, let's do it."

Just a few blocks into their run, Bridget was unsure whether she could keep up. She felt so hot it was like being inside a volcano, and with each stride, her stomach churned. Bridget felt her forehead with the back of her hand. Maybe she had a fever. Bridget pressed the button on her FitLife for an update.

"Miles to goal: Two-point-zero."

Bridget knew there was no way she'd be able to run two more miles this morning. Maybe she could get a couple in later today.

Carmina tapped Bridget's arm with a sweaty hand.

"Look strong," she said. "We're going past Mark and his friends."

Bridget could see the boys playing basketball up ahead. She didn't know why Carmina cared so much. Mark probably wouldn't even notice them again. But Bridget attempted to straighten up and lengthened her stride.

Then something weird happened.

The churning in Bridget's stomach got worse—a lot worse. Bridget skidded to a stop as Carmina continued on. Bridget leaned over and, gripping her knees, vomited all over the path.

In the distance, she heard Carmina shout, "Oh no!"

Shaking, Bridget straightened to see that Mark and all the other boys were, for once, looking their way.

8

A New Pace

Bridget could've died of embarrassment. She couldn't believe that she'd thrown up in front of the most popular guy in school and all his friends.

"Gross!" one of Mark's friends said.

"That's nasty," another said.

"Hey there!" Mark yelled. "You okay? Want me to call someone for ya?"

Carmina was already at Bridget's side. "She's fine. I've got her." To Bridget she said, "Are you okay? Do you need to sit down?"

Bridget felt deflated. Now that she wasn't trying to convince herself she was okay, she realized how sick she really was.

"Yeah," Bridget said. "I need a drink."

Carmina led Bridget to a bench away from the boys. "I guess we finally got Mark's attention," she joked.

For some reason, this just made Bridget feel even worse. Who wanted to get a boy's attention by vomiting? It was horrific. She buried her sweaty face in her hands.

"At least he didn't get too close," Bridget said, nearly sobbing. "I have throw-up breath."

Carmina patted her back. "Hey, hey, it's okay. I was just joking. I thought you didn't look right this morning. You must be really sick."

Bridget sniffled. "Yeah, I think I must have the flu."

"Look, I know you love soccer, and you want to improve," Carmina said finally. "But you have to take it easy on yourself."

Bridget sighed. "I know. I know." She looked at her bracelet. "I got caught up using the FitLife and competing with you. I mean, I probably have a fever right now, and I didn't even notice. But I . . . I want to be the best forward on the team. And I'm jealous because you are," Bridget admitted.

Carmina shook her head. "But that's just not true. I might be faster than you, but you have way better control of the ball. Coach even said that to me. He said he was glad we were working out together because then maybe the team would have two star forwards this year."

Astonished, Bridget stared at Carmina. "Really? He said that?"

"Yes! In fact, I've been meaning to ask you if you'd like to help me with my foot skills."

"Definitely," Bridget smiled. Her head pounded. "But right now, I feel awful."

Carmina laughed. "Really?"

"I'm gonna call my dad and have him come get me," Bridget said. She sighed, knowing that at least this time, both her dad and Emma had been right in their concern for her.

"Okay," Carmina said. Then, after a pause, she asked "Are you going to keep using FitLife?"

Bridget thought about it for a minute. "Yeah, I am," Bridget said. "But from now on, I'm going to remember to set my own pace."

The End

Think About It

1. Examine the characters who interact with Bridget throughout the story: Bridget's dad, Coach Harrison, Carmina, Emma, and Poua. Describe how each person influenced, or tried to influence, Bridget's actions. Did some have a positive influence while others had a negative one?

2. Do you feel it was right for Bridget to stop training with Emma? If you were Bridget, how would you have handled the situation?

3. Read another Bridget Gadget story and compare it to *Fitness Crash*. How does Bridget's focus on a tech gadget cause her trouble in each story? How are her problems the same? How are they different? Use examples from the books to support your answer.

Write About It

1. Gadgets such as the FitLife bracelet can help people accomplish tasks and goals. What tech products do you use in your everyday life? Which do you think are most helpful to people? Make a list of these gadgets and describe how they benefit people who use them.

2. In this story, Bridget depends too heavily on her gadget and forgets to listen to her own body. Have you ever been so absorbed with a tech gadget that you lost track of the world around you? What happened? Write a story about it.

3. In this story, Bridget wants to be the star forward on her soccer team. Have you ever wanted to be the best at something? Write a story about it. What was your goal, and how did you try to achieve it? Did you succeed? If you not, did you at least improve?

About the Author

Mari Kesselring is a writer and editor of books for young people. She's written on various subjects, including William Shakespeare, Franklin D. Roosevelt, and the attack on Pearl Harbor. She is currently pursuing a Master of Fine Arts in Creative Writing at Hamline University. Like Bridget, Mari enjoys technology and new gadgets. She appreciates how technology provides unlimited access to knowledge and brings people closer together. Mari lives in St. Paul, Minnesota, with her husband and their dog, Lady.

About the Illustrator

Mariano Epelbaum has illustrated books for publishers in the United States, Puerto Rico, Spain, and Argentina. He has also worked as an animator for commercials, television shows, and movies, such as *Pantriste*, *Micaela*, and *Manuelita*. Mariano was also the art director and character designer for *Underdogs*, an animated movie about foosball. He currently lives in Buenos Aires, Argentina.

More Fun with Bridget Gadget

Digital Reveal
Bridget secretly writes a review of TechPaper, a paper-thin tablet that her dad's company is developing. No one is supposed to know about the device yet. But that all changes when Bridget's post with pictures of the device goes viral.

Drone Detective
Bridget begins to wonder if her friends Emma and Eric are dating. When she uses a research drone to spy on them, the secret that she discovers isn't the one she thought her friends were keeping.

Pixel Perfection
Bridget and Emma are surprised by the attention they receive after the launch of their e-zine, *Cyber Hills Holler*. However, when they start editing photos of their classmates to retain their new-found popularity, not everyone is happy with the results.

READ MORE FROM 12-STORY LIBRARY